EDGE
BOOKS™

DRAGONS

REAL-LIFE
DRAGONS

by Matt Doeden

Consultant
Dr. Peter Hogarth
Professor, Department of Biology
University of York, United Kingdom

Capstone
press®

Mankato, Minnesota

Edge Books are published by Capstone Press,
151 Good Counsel Drive, P.O. Box 669, Mankato, Minnesota 56002.
www.capstonepress.com

Library of Congress Cataloging-in-Publication Data
Doeden, Matt.
   Real-life dragons / by Matt Doeden.
      p. cm. — (Edge books. Dragons)
      Summary: "Describes real-life animals and their similarities to
dragons" — Provided by publisher.
      Includes bibliographical references and index.
      ISBN–13: 978-1-4296-1296-8 (hardcover)
      ISBN–10: 1-4296-1296-7 (hardcover)
      1. Animals — Juvenile literature. 2. Dragons — Juvenile literature.
3. Comparison (Philosophy) — Juvenile literature. I. Title. II. Series.
QL49.D616 2008
590 — dc22   2007025096

Editorial Credits

Aaron Sautter, editor; Ted Williams, designer; Richard Pellegrino, illustrator;
   Jo Miller, photo researcher

Photo Credits

Alamy/Images & Stories, 18
BigStockPhoto.com/plastique, 29
Corbis/Reuters/George Mulala, 26–27; Solus-Veer/Sam Forencich, 25;
   Wolfgang Kaehler, 14
Dreamstime/Krzysztof Gorski, 21
Mary Evans Picture Library, 24
Peter Arnold/John R. MacGregor, 19
Photo Researchers, Inc, 13; Mark Garlick, 11
Sculpture and Photo © 2006 The Children's Museum of
   Indianapolis/Sculpture by Victor Porter, 8
Shutterstock/abzora, backgrounds; Andrey Zyk, backgrounds;
   Johan Swanepoel, 20; Tony Wear, 16–17

1 2 3 4 5 6 13 12 11 10 09 08

Table of Contents

CHAPTER ONE

A Mystery In Stone

Imagine two peasants traveling on a narrow mountain path hundreds of years ago. It's a hot summer day. The peasants sit down near a couple of large boulders to rest.

One of the peasants notices something odd nearby. It's a strange shape in the rock. Together, the peasants clear away some loose gravel and stones. They've just found a dinosaur skeleton.

But the peasants are poor and uneducated. They can't imagine what sort of beast the bones might have belonged to. Fearing the unknown, they cry out, "It's dragon bones!"

The peasants gather their things and leave in a hurry. They want to put as much distance as they can between themselves and the bones. Who knows what sort of dangerous magic the bones might contain?

Where Do Legends Begin?

Legends about fearsome creatures like dragons often begin with a grain of truth. What would these peasants have thought about the dinosaur bones? They probably would have known very little about science or history. Their imaginations might have run wild. Perhaps someone from the village disappeared long ago. Maybe that person was a victim of a dragon! New dragon legends often grew out of the stories people told about such events.

Stories about dragons are found all over the world. How could people from so many **cultures** create such similar beasts? Did they see dinosaur bones? Did living animals such as lizards or crocodiles inspire these myths? Or was there something more? We can never really be sure. But it's fun to imagine what the truth might be.

culture – the way of life, customs, and traditions of a group of people

Frightened peasants probably told wild stories about things they didn't understand.

7

Dracorex hogwartsia was a dinosaur that looked a lot like a real dragon.

Chapter Two

Prehistoric Beasts

Millions of years ago, dinosaurs ruled the Earth. These great reptiles may be what inspired the idea of dragons. Dinosaurs were huge and powerful. Many had long, sharp teeth and tough, armorlike skin. After dinosaurs died, many of their bones were preserved in rock. Today, we know these fossils were once dinosaurs. But we can only imagine what ancient people thought of them.

Dozens of dinosaur **species** may have resembled dragons. The stegosaurus had large plates of armor running up and down its back. In 2003, a previously unknown dinosaur was found in South Dakota. The dinosaur, named dracorex hogwartsia, had a skull that looked much like a dragon's. But of all the ancient reptiles, the tyrannosaurus rex and pterosaurs may have been the most dragonlike.

species – a group of animals with similar features

The Tyrannosaurus Rex

It's easy to imagine the mighty tyrannosaurus rex as a prehistoric dragon. These large, powerful dinosaurs struck terror into their prey. In fact, their name means "king tyrant lizard."

The tyrannosaurus rex was one of the largest meateaters ever to live. These monsters often grew up to 50 feet (15 meters) long from head to tail. The skull alone could measure 5 feet (1.5 meters) long. Their teeth were up to 7 inches (18 centimeters) long, but they didn't always need them. They probably swallowed smaller animals whole. It's not hard to imagine what ancient people may have thought of a tyrannosaurus rex skeleton. Give the creature a pair of wings and fiery breath, and you have a vicious dragon.

Tyrannosaurus rex was a vicious hunter.

Pterosaurs

With pterosaurs, you don't even need to imagine wings. These big flying reptiles already had them. There were many kinds of pterosaurs. Some had wingspans as wide as 40 feet (12 meters). Pterosaurs had long, narrow heads, large eyes, and small, razor-sharp teeth. They likely swooped down out of the sky to catch their prey. If people saw a pterosaur in flight today, they would probably think it looked like a dragon.

DRAGON FACT

Many scientists think a huge asteroid killed the dinosaurs. The dust created by the impact changed Earth's climate so they could no longer survive.

Pterosaurs probably looked a lot like dragons flying through the sky.

Komodo dragons are some of today's largest and deadliest reptiles.

CHAPTER THREE

Dragons Among Us

You don't have to travel back in time to find dragonlike creatures on Earth. Maybe dragon stories didn't come from dinosaurs at all. It's possible that more modern animals inspired legends about dragons.

Reptiles

Dinosaurs no longer roam the planet hunting prey. But smaller reptiles are found everywhere. One of the most dragonlike creatures lives in Indonesia. Komodo dragons are the world's largest lizards. They can grow up to 10 feet (3 meters) long. They often weigh as much as 300 pounds (136 kilograms) or more. With long tails and razor-sharp teeth, these modern lizards really earn the name dragon.

Leafy sea dragons look a lot like mythical dragons.

Alligators and crocodiles also remind people of dragons. The Chinese alligator strongly resembles pictures of Asian dragons. Legends say Asian dragons were long and thin and spent much of their time in water. Chinese alligators share many of these qualities.

DRAGON FACT

One of the largest crocodiles ever reported lived in India. The big beast was nearly 23 feet (7 meters) long.

Other Animals

Reptiles aren't the only dragonlike creatures sharing our world today. From the sea to the sky, creatures that remind people of dragons are everywhere.

The oceans are filled with creatures that look like dragons. The sea dragon is a rare type of fish that lives off the coast of Australia. Sea dragons are closely related to seahorses. About 14 inches (36 centimeters) long, they look like tiny swimming dragons.

Dragon moray eels are very aggressive.

Moray eels have a fearsome appearance. These long, skinny fish use their sharp teeth to capture and kill their prey. One of the rarest moray eels is the dragon moray. Dragon morays live near tropical islands in the southern Pacific Ocean. These brightly colored fish have horns just above their large eyes. Dragon morays don't just appear fierce, though. They're very aggressive and will attack almost anything, including people.

Giant Pacific salamanders make their homes in freshwater instead of the ocean. These huge **amphibians** can grow up to 6 feet (2 meters) long. They have long, flexible bodies with tough, thick skin. Giant salamanders live mainly in small rivers or streams in Japan and China. These strange creatures may have helped inspire stories of water dragons in Asia.

> **amphibian** – a cold-blooded animal that can live both in water and on land

Giant Pacific salamanders may have inspired some Asian dragon legends.

The sky is also filled with creatures that remind people of dragons. Many scientists believe dinosaurs were the **ancestors** of modern birds. Vultures and other birds with large wings often remind people of big soaring dragons.

ancestor – a family member who lived a long time ago

Vultures have a very large wingspan.

Dragonflies are some of the largest and fastest flying insects in the world.

Dragonflies also make people think of mythical dragons. Dragonflies use great speed to capture mosquitoes and other prey. Dragonflies come in many sizes and colors. The largest dragonflies have wingspans more than 7 inches (18 centimeters) wide. Dragonflies live all over the world. You may even see these little dragons in your own backyard.

Chapter Four

Mythical Beasts

Today we know dragons are just imaginary creatures. There's no reason to believe the fire-breathing beasts were ever real. Even dinosaurs weren't really dragons. Still, why are dragon stories told all over the world? Could some dragonlike beast have survived into modern times?

Dragon Fact

Stories about dragons are found on every continent on earth. Some legends are more than 3,700 years old!

Long ago, sailors told many stories of giant sea serpents.

Real or Imagined?

Sailors once believed dragons lived in the oceans. They often told tales of sea serpents that terrorized and attacked their ships. Could a living creature have inspired these legends? Or did the stories come from someone's imagination? Perhaps these ancient sea dragons were simply whales, sharks, or giant squids.

Some people believe the Loch Ness monster in Scotland is a real creature. People have claimed to see the monster, nicknamed Nessie, for hundreds of years. Since 1934, several blurry photos and videos have been taken of something in the lake. But so far, no one has been able to find real proof of the monster.

Many people believe that Nessie is a real creature.

Many people think Nessie is really a plesiosaur that somehow survived to the present day. Plesiosaurs were large swimming reptiles that lived at the time of the dinosaurs. Critics point out that like the dinosaurs, plesiosaurs have been **extinct** for millions of years. But Nessie's believers point to another ancient creature.

extinct – no longer living anywhere in the world

Several coelacanth fish have been found since 1938.

The coelacanth is an ancient fish that people thought died out about the same time as the dinosaurs. But in 1938, one was found off the coast of Madagascar. If the fish species survived millions of years, is it possible plesiosaurs survived as well? It's not likely, but the possibility fascinates believers.

Where Are The Dragons?

It's fun to imagine that dragons are real. If they were, where would they live? Nobody has ever seen a dragon, so they'd have to be well hidden. A few places on Earth haven't been explored very well. Maybe dragons live near the ocean floor. Or maybe they live in deep underground caves.

Could dragons survive at the Earth's poles? Could they live high in the Himalayan Mountains? It doesn't seem likely. But that doesn't stop people's imaginations from running wild. Tales of dragons have been around for thousands of years. They'll probably be with us for a long time to come.

DRAGON FACT

Some people keep dragons as pets! Frilled dragons and bearded dragons are popular pets among lizard lovers.

Dragons are popular imaginary creatures all over the world.

Glossary

amphibian (am-FI-bee-uhn) — a cold-blooded animal with a backbone; amphibians live in water when young, and can live on land as an adult.

ancestor (AN-ses-tuhr) — a member of a family or species who lived a long time ago

coelacanth (SEE-luh-kanth) — an ancient fish species that was thought to be extinct

culture (KUHL-chuhr) — the way of life, customs, and traditions of a group of people

extinct (ik-STINGKT) — no longer living anywhere in the world

peasant (PEZ-uhnt) — a poor person in Europe who worked on a farm or owned a small farm

plesiosaur (PLEE-see-uh-sohr) — a large swimming reptile that lived during the time of the dinosaurs

species (SPEE-sheez) — a group of animals or plants that share common characteristics

Read More

Dixon, Dougal, and John Malam. *Dinosaur*. E. Guides. New York: DK, 2004.

Gresko, Marcia S. *Komodo Dragons. Nature's Predators.* San Diego: Kidhaven Press, 2004.

Krensky, Stephen. *Dragons*. Monster Chronicles. Minneapolis: Lerner, 2007.

Internet Sites

FactHound offers a safe, fun way to find Internet sites related to this book. All of the sites on FactHound have been researched by our staff.

Here's how:
1. Visit *www.facthound.com*
2. Choose your grade level.
3. Type in this book ID **1429612967** for age-appropriate sites. You may also browse subjects by clicking on letters, or by clicking on pictures and words.
4. Click on the **Fetch It** button.

FactHound will fetch the best sites for you!

INDEX